SHAPES

Shelley Rotner and Anne Woodhull
Photographs by Shelley Rotner

Holiday House   New York

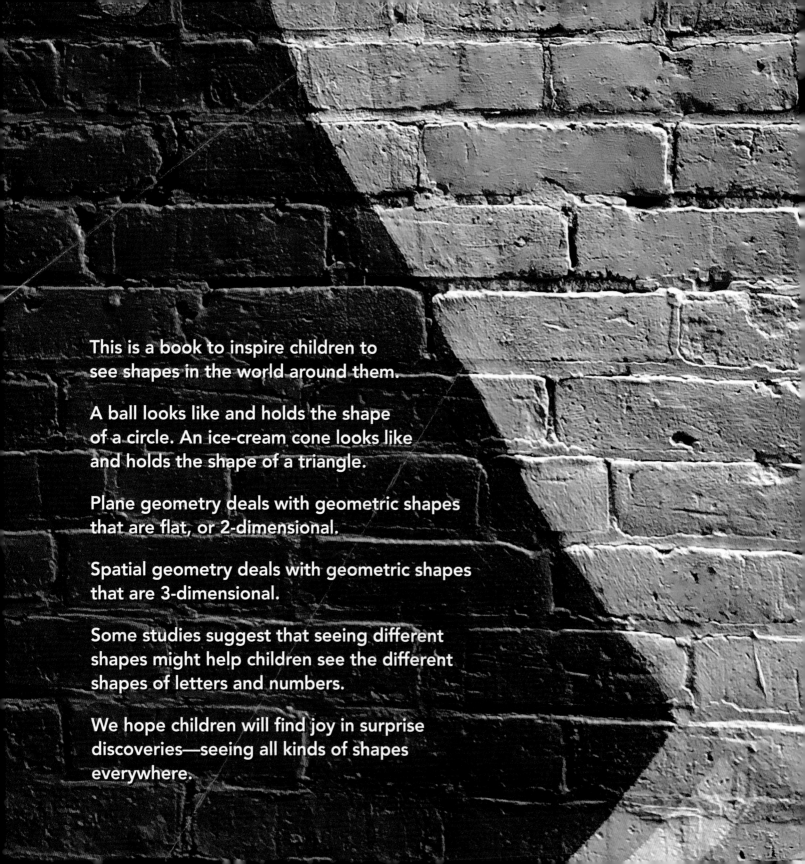

This is a book to inspire children to
see shapes in the world around them.

A ball looks like and holds the shape
of a circle. An ice-cream cone looks like
and holds the shape of a triangle.

Plane geometry deals with geometric shapes
that are flat, or 2-dimensional.

Spatial geometry deals with geometric shapes
that are 3-dimensional.

Some studies suggest that seeing different
shapes might help children see the different
shapes of letters and numbers.

We hope children will find joy in surprise
discoveries—seeing all kinds of shapes
everywhere.

Dedicated to Sheila Kelly

**For her depth and breadth
and significant understanding
of the worlds of children.**

Special thanks to Katie Craig for
her design of this book.

Text copyright © 2019 by Shelley Rotner and
Anne Woodhull
Photos copyright © 2019 by Shelley Rotner
All Rights Reserved
HOLIDAY HOUSE is registered in the U.S. Patent
and Trademark Office.
Printed and bound in March 2020 at Toppan
Leefung, DongGuan City, China.
www.holidayhouse.com
First Edition
1 3 5 7 9 10 8 6 4 2
Library of Congress Cataloging-in-Publication Data
Names: Rotner, Shelley, author.
Woodhull, Anne Love, author.
Title: Shapes / Shelley Rotner, Anne Woodhull.
Description: First edition. | New York : Holiday
house, [2020] | Audience:
Ages 2-5 | Audience: Pre-school,
excluding K | Summary: "An introduction
to shapes with examples of real-life
objects that resemble those
shapes"—Provided by publisher.
Identifiers: LCCN 2019020317
ISBN 9780823446384 (hardcover)
Subjects: LCSH: Shapes—Juvenile
literature.
Classification: LCC QA482 .R68
2020 | DDC 516/.15—dc23
LC record available at
https://lccn.loc.gov/2019020317

CiRCLES
fl°at...

Polka dots, peas,
a ball.
Owl eyes.
Lollipops and clocks.
Marbles, the moon
and sun.

TRIANGLES

chime...

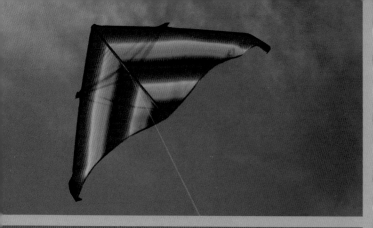

Kites and sailboats.
Ice-cream cones and
party hats.
Quilts,
pizza.
Pumpkin eyes.

SQUARES

build...

Chocolate, checkers, chess.
Ice cubes.
Puzzles and presents.
Hopscotch.

RECTANGLES

play...

Trains, buses,
trucks, and books.
Bricks, buildings,
windows, and flags.

OVALS

pOp...

Eggs, grapes,
lemons, and leaves.
Jellybeans, seeds,
sunglasses.
A spoon.

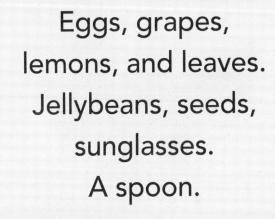

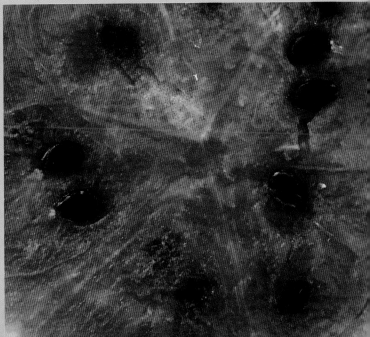

DIAMONDS fly

Cards,
baseball diamonds,
tiles, and textiles.
Signs
and building designs.

STARS

bloom

Cookies, clothes,
barrettes, and flags.
Starfish and star fruit,
stickers, and spice.

What shapes
do you see?